I0520296

HEART OF PALMS

A Novella

Holly L Aasen

Serealities Press
www.serealities.com

Copyright © 2014 Holly L Aasen

All rights reserved.

Cover Image: Mayer George/Shutterstock

ISBN: 0692281800

ISBN 13: 9780692281802

Library of Congress Control Number: 2014916006

Serealities Press, Birmingham AL

Contents

1

The Verdict

The verdict was in. After spending months in jail, Cole Wells was found not guilty of drug trafficking.

As he walked out of the Oak Hill Courthouse into bright sunlight, he looked down at the audience of reporters, photographers, police, curious strangers, and admirers. Soon after his arrest, a fan club, largely made up of young college girls, emerged—the *Free Cole Coalition*. Bright white T-shirts covered the sidewalk below.

The girls who formed this fan club were adamant that he had to be innocent. Just look at him. Cole was not merely handsome, but stunningly beautiful. Chiseled features with heavily lashed, large blue eyes and a mop of sandy-blond hair that gave him a messy, rugged quality. He was tall with a muscular athlete's frame and big, solid arms any girl would want wrapped around her.

His charm and good looks paved the way to many dates with numerous girls. Girls were always throwing themselves at him, but he struggled to get past the first couple of dates with any of them. Most of the girls found his limited intellect frustrating. They were anxious to sleep with him, but none of them held an interest for long in him. They just couldn't handle such limited conversations and his strange behavior. He would often start a story, stop midsentence, and switch to something entirely different. His thoughts were disconnected. Frequently, awkward things would just spew out of his mouth with no direction.

Some of his actions were also hard for the girls to understand. Once, on a rare third date, he gave a girl a small, beautifully wrapped box. Inside it, she found a dead spider. He explained that because she had told him how much she hated spiders, he thought she would be thrilled if he brought a dead one to her. That would be their last date.

Although his teachers had always found him "special," no one could ever find quite the right diagnosis or label for him, as he functioned at a fairly reasonable level. His athletic skills and low IQ tested that was just on the borderline to be considered mildly handicapped, qualified him to compete in the Special Olympics. This became an important part of his life which started around age twelve. His good looks helped him even become quite a local celebrity, a spokesperson and champion of the charity, for which he helped raise money and promoted events.

His father, Jack Wells, had encouraged the Special Olympics involvement early on. He and Cole even trained together to keep up his fitness routine. Now at age twenty-three, Cole lived alone in an apartment, but he and Jack would meet at the gym and hang out together. Cole had been so much a part of his father's life. Now, Jack couldn't understand how they had gotten to this point on this beautiful day in front of the crowd facing the courthouse. Jack was a detective, and he had reached a conclusion in sharp contrast to that of the judge, the jury, his fellow officers, and all of those adoring fans: Cole should have been found guilty.

Jack had originally thought his son would only be charged with drug possession. Generally, this would mean a slap-on-the-wrist for a first time offender, particularly, given his mental challenges. However, Oak Hill was a conservative Midwestern, mid-sized city. In recent years drugs like meth and heroin had become more widespread. Just a few weeks prior to his arrest, two young 8th grade boys were found dead of a heroin overdose under the bleachers in their school. Mothers, fathers and families of Oak Hill were outraged. Politicians looked to capitalize on this outrage since election time was drawing near. They vowed to crack down hard without exception. Cole's arrest would send a signal that no one was exempt. The combination of drugs and large amount of cash found in his backpack qualified him for the trafficking charge.

As Cole took his first step down into that admiring crowd, he flashed his father a grin and a wink. Jack was filled with all of the emotion from the trial—the disappointment, the betrayal, and the disbelief that his only son and his best friend could have actually been selling drugs. The wink was like a stab to the heart. It was as if Cole knew he was getting away with something. Jack couldn't contain his anger. In one swift move, he launched his fist straight into that winking eye. Cole stumbled backward over the step behind him, and his head smacked the concrete. He then rolled down the steps like a rag doll, stopping right at the feet of the reporters.

Dozens of cameras kept rolling, capturing every second as the blood began to ooze from Cole's head. The hottest story of the year in Oak Hill had taken a crazy, violent turn. The reporters couldn't have been more shocked. They had been following the story since Cole's initial arrest and featuring his close relationship with his father. They had been waiting to capture an emotional hug, a trickle of manly tears, or a joyful embrace celebrating the verdict.

Denny Nolan was one of the cameramen on the scene. Without flinching, he kept the camera rolling. The instinct to get the story overtook his instinct to help as Cole's head hit the pavement right below his feet. He loved being behind the camera and capturing video was his art. His true talent was in looking at things in a different way, from a slightly different angle, and a different perspective than the average cameraman. He challenged himself to see the scene in front of him, as well as the things around the scene.

He knew he had to keep filming. He focused on keeping steady. A camera had been glued to his hands since he was eight years old. He rarely put it down, especially now that his career depended on it. He thought someone in the crowd would surely call 911, and there had to be public safety personnel nearby. Someone would take care of the situation, but Denny wondered why it had even happened. *Why did Cole's dad snap like that?*

2

Doctor's Report

Jack had immediately left the scene enraged, shocked at his own actions and angry at himself. With television stations and newspapers clamoring for access to the vast camera footage that would likely be available, the police would likely have to arrest one of their own but at the moment, they too were in shock. No one knew what Jack had discovered about Cole before the verdict.

At the hospital, Dr. Ella Stanton was the neurologist on call when paramedics called to say they were en route with a head trauma patient. She had gone into adrenaline overdrive when she learned that patient was Cole. Her sister had gone to high school with him, and she had followed the family's sad story in the aftermath of Cole's mother's death.

Ella pushed those thoughts aside when Cole arrived and devoted herself entirely to the task before her. She had to perform emergency surgery to reduce the swelling in Cole's brain and to minimize additional damage to the brain tissue. She would need to open a window in the skull to reduce pressure by providing space for swelling tissue. To do this, she would have to put him into a temporary, medically induced coma. Ella knew that once she finished the long surgery, she would have to be thorough in her reporting. The press would want answers. They would demand full disclosure of his medical condition in the wake of a trial that had ended so violently and mysteriously.

She thought back to Cole's mother, Meredith, who had died in a freak accident when he was just ten years old. An avid runner, she usually went out each morning to run along a canal as the sun rose. One day, on the bridge above the path where she was running, an eighteen-wheeler blew a tire. A piece of rubber shrapnel flew through the air and hit her neck with such speed and force, it decapitated her.

The accident that took Meredith's life was so bizarre. Big trucks were always blowing tires, but the shredded rubber usually settled on or near the road without causing harm. Her death seemed like a cruel and unusual punishment from the heavens. It was as if she had been handpicked to die that day. The truck driver never even knew what happened, and the blown tire went undetected for several miles. There were no witnesses and Meredith's headless body lay by the canal until the next runner who came by that morning happened upon the gory scene.

A uniformed officer at the time, Jack always left for his shift after she returned. That morning, she never returned. Another officer he knew came by to give him the news. He had seen horrific amounts of blood and tragic death in his line of work, but nothing compared to the effect of that moment. He never saw the body. He never even saw photos from the scene, but the gruesome nature of her death would haunt him relentlessly. He was never the same after that day.

At first, he could hardly even care for Cole. He had no family in town but he was close to many of the other officers. They would often come by and check on him, offer to help, and bring food. Eventually though, as life went on, the visits tapered off, and Jack did not welcome anyone new into his life. His mind was his enemy, and his anger only grew in the months following her death. He was never a religious man, but the cruelty of his wife's death provided certainty that God did not exist. At some level, however, Jack knew that only a higher power could create such a beautiful life and take it away so easily.

Jack began to believe in God only to blame and rage against Him. He started drinking heavily, and the alcohol freed his desire to scream and curse God. He became more and more dependent on the bottle as his pain worsened.

Cole was never the same either. Before the loss of his mother, he was a bright and happy child. He was always smiling and loved to simply play with his Legos more than anything. He didn't excel at schoolwork, but his teachers had no reason to think there was anything wrong with him. After his mother's death, Cole became more and more despondent. He wouldn't speak much. Jack would continue drinking long after sending Cole to bed. Cole would listen to his father screaming at God, and it scared him. He slept with a pillow over his ears to drown out the sound. His grades slipped so far, he was held back that year in school. His behavior became more erratic and he had difficulty focusing on anything at all. The school psychologist eventually ordered an evaluation after a year of his continuing decline. His teachers knew about the tragedy, so they tried to give him extra help and made no demands on him. However, state law required him to pass standardized tests. When he performed so poorly, they had to intervene. The psychologist believed that Cole had perhaps always had a borderline low IQ and that maybe his parents and teachers didn't realize it until his education became more advanced in school. But he also believed that Cole had been so severely traumatized that it stunted his mental and emotional capacity. He was then declared mentally challenged and required to attend remedial classes at his school.

This was a wake-up call for Jack and he began to pull himself back together as he recognized how much his son needed him. He quit drinking, joined Alcoholics Anonymous, and lifted himself out of the fog. His rage against God shrank to mere resentment. His realization of the full extent of Cole's dependence on him gave him a reason to live that made sense when nothing else did. He knew he had to take care of Cole, the most precious remnant of his dear Meredith. He began to coach track-and-field for their local Special Olympics chapter because he wanted Cole to stay active and healthy. He worked hard for the charity, and it provided an outlet for him to stay busy in a productive way that made a difference.

3

A Father's Remorse

Ella saw the hospital administrator waving to her as he came down the hall. There would be a press conference in an hour. She expected to be included as a spokesperson. Just then, her phone rang. She was shocked to hear Cole's father on the other end. As Jack confirmed his identity, Ella waved to the administrator, who signaled that he didn't need to interrupt as he handed her the outline for the press conference and left.

"How did you get my number?" she asked Jack.

"Well I'm a detective," he said. "Listen, I only have a few minutes, and I can't come to the hospital. I know he's in a coma, and I know you'll be taking care of him. What's his prognosis?"

Ella explained the surgery and emphasized that she would likely be able to pull him out of the coma in just a few days.

"Don't tell anyone I contacted you," Jack continued. "I want to know everything about his progress, and I'll give you instructions soon on how to contact me. If you tell anyone, and I mean anyone, there will be serious consequences."

Jack paused. Then, he said slowly and emphatically, "I will tell you more later, but I need to trust you. Do you understand? Can I count on you?"

"I...I think so. I mean, yes, of course. But the police are probably going to be looking for you."

"I'm not worried about that. They won't be looking too hard, but you have to keep quiet so I can talk to you—so you can help Cole. I want him to get better, even if he's not the son I thought he was," he mumbled. "Just please take care of him." And with that last request, Jack hung up and Ella was left to wonder many things about what she should do next and why he called her directly.

"Stay focused," Ella muttered to herself. She decided it was more important to get answers from Jack than to contact the police—and she needed to get ready for the press conference. She was nervous but excited about her first media appearance.

4

Psychic Readings

While Ella was preparing for the press conference, her sister Lily was on the other side of town preparing for an important event of her own. Just the day before, she had finally received the call she had been anticipating for several months. She had made it through the initial interviews and would be singing for the regional round of *American Idol*. This round would feature the first level of competitors in their hometowns. Fifteen contestants from Oak Hill would be competing, and this special edition would spotlight a particular charity in each town. Her town would focus on the Special Olympics. Cole had originally been a featured speaker for the charity since he was such a local favorite and well-known participant.

Lily's planning for this opportunity required an emergency meeting at the home of her psychic advisor, Ivy Keller, without whom Lily could not possibly make her most important decisions. Her critical decision today was what color dress to wear for the audition. Yes, Lily's worries in life were small in comparison to the rest of the world. She lived a carefree, easy life but each detail of this upcoming night would be most critical to her.

As Lily waited patiently, Ivy closed her eyes and thought for a bit. Then, she gave her answer, "Green…it will be a brilliant green like emeralds in the sunlight. Not a soft shade of green but a strong, magnificent green." Lily frowned. She didn't like the answer.

"But, um, are you really sure? Are you sure you see a green color?" Lily asked. "I was thinking red might be exciting. Something more dramatic! Wouldn't red appear better on camera?" Lily spoke hesitantly, knowing she shouldn't question Ivy.

Ivy's eyes widened. Her expression was one of disapproval. "Do you not understand me, my little Lily? Do you not understand how important this is for you?" Ivy asked.

She had always called her "my little Lily" as they had been so close ever since Lily was a little girl. Several times a year, beginning on her fifth birthday, her mother, Veronica, brought both of her daughters, Ella and Lily, to Ivy for palm readings. Ivy had helped advise and guide them throughout their lives.

As Ella found success through her studies and medical school, she didn't put much stock in the visions of her mother's friend, the psychic. She was much more skeptical by nature than Lily, who had continued to seek Ivy's guidance on everything from dating to friendships to the selection of her college courses. Without Ivy, Lily feared she would be lost and wandering this great big world without a GPS, so she quickly dismissed her initial doubtfulness. "I'm sorry, yes, of course—green! I'll go shopping today. I will find the most fabulous green dress. I'll even bring it to show you this evening!" she said enthusiastically, hoping to atone for questioning Ivy's judgment.

"But, yes, you understand, and you will see…you will see. It is all right here within your reach…now. With all of the hard work you face, the rewards will be granted to you in return! Now, focus!" Lily jumped. "This is just the beginning. Never forget that you must succeed. You will win, and you will gain fame beyond what you can even dream. Everything I have prepared you for will come to be."

Ivy grasped Lily's hands firmly. Ivy's hands were always cold, with thick blue veins pulsing and skin that was always ever so soft. Ivy knew that the hands could tell so much about a person beyond what she read in their palms. Other features: nails, rings, veins, cuticles, wrinkles, and freckles—each told parts of the life story. She paid close attention to all parts of the external shell of a person. All that was visible could give her clues to the status of health, character, mind, and motivation.

5

Beyond the Palms

The words *Palm Reader* glowed on the neon sign in the window. Ivy promoted herself as such among Oak Hill's elite for all practical purposes. That was a term people could easily understand, although, in reality, she was far more than just a common street psychic. She held a doctorate in metaphysics and had devoted her life to the continued studies of philosophy, religion, astrology, and holistic healing, while also building her skills in the realms of numerology, colorology, and even psychology. She was meticulous in her studies and able to bring together all of these principles in order to gain a complete understanding of her clients and to give them superior guidance.

Ivy used her talents and wisdom to help her clients choose the right paths. She was not interested in those who came to her seeking to understand the past. She was not there to talk about previous lives or to debate the merits of her clients' previous decisions in their current lives. She used all of her powers and knowledge strictly for future guidance. She would accept only clients who were committed to listening and following the powers of the universe.

Ivy's services were not cheap, but she was easily able to convince her clients, her very wealthy clients in particular, that knowledge is power, and knowledge beyond the purely physical world is how one could attain supreme power. Her knowledge of the power of the stars, moon phases, solar energy, color, and numeric calculations impressed her clients and led them to believe they existed at a higher level than normal people. They trusted her implicitly. Her intellect, combined with her powers of perception and persuasion, made Ivy a powerful and intimidating woman.

Ivy's unusual beauty struck people. She was nearly six feet tall—thin with milky skin and shoulder-length, deep-auburn hair that made her eyes even more dazzling. Referring to herself as a palm reader was the easiest way to fit into a category people could understand. Her abilities were her means to an income, and her income was dependent on her clients' dedication. Their success equaled her success. She had to first gain a client's complete trust; then she insisted on their commitment to following her guidance. Each client had to fulfill her rigorous requirements in order to maintain her counsel.

Ivy watched through the large bay window as Lily exited her house. She had big plans for Lily. Her little Lily would be the key to Ivy's success, yet Lily had no idea that Ivy's entire life's work and future were dependent on her rise to fame.

6

The Power of Five

Lily walked swiftly to her car, a sleek Jaguar convertible. She checked her phone for messages and saw nothing from her boyfriend, Denny, about the trial. She knew Denny would have his hands glued to the camera as usual. She was curious about Cole's trial but far more consumed with preparations for her own event.

This audition would be Lily's moment to shine. Her older sister was the smart one. It was hard to compete with a brain surgeon and impossible for her to trump Ella's brilliance. She believed the only way to success was through her talent. This would be her big break and her opportunity to finally be recognized. Singing came naturally to her. She had an ear for music and a distinct voice. It was a strong and soulful voice she couldn't wait to bring to a national stage.

Lily enjoyed seeing Ivy, and she trusted her completely. She often wished her own mother could be more like Ivy. Her mother, Veronica, was more interested in business than in nurturing or helping her children. Lily knew her mother loved her, but she felt her appreciation was akin to what one would feel for a piece of property. She knew her mother could never truly be there for her emotionally. If Veronica ever had to choose between her daughters and the company, Lily knew the company would always win. It was her passion.

As Lily left Ivy's house seeking the perfect green dress, she felt a chill in the spring air. That was unusual for the time of year, and it made her think about the color Ivy had instructed her to wear. *Green mermaids, lizards, and dinos…Oh my!*

With her long, dark hair and petite frame, she thought green would overpower her, but through all of life's biggest decisions, Ivy's advice was always correct. She had taught her to pay attention to numbers, moon phases, dates, and yes, even colors that would contribute to the successes and failures in her life.

Following Ivy's guidance had led Lily to understand some of the powers beyond the purely physical world and to uncover the universal spiritual forces that could help her. Numbers were highly important, as she had discovered, and the number five was her special good luck charm. Ivy taught her that the number five was directly related to the creation of the universe.

All things happen in fives, or they are divisible by five. She believed everything was directly or indirectly linked to the number five. It could be found everywhere, even in the human body with its five fingers, five toes, and five senses. She revered it as the number of harmony and balance.

This important event happened to fall beautifully into place. She had an almost perfect alignment. The date of the event was May 23. May was the fifth month, the digits in twenty-three added up to five, and it would be the fifth full moon of the year on that night. The name of the color Ivy had chosen—green— was composed of five letters. It was no coincidence. This would definitely be her moment.

7

The Power of Chaos

As Lily prepared for her shining moment, Ivy prepared for her life's work to come to fruition. She was meticulous about tracking Lily's progress. Every aspect of her research had to be documented in her journal.

Lily came to visit me today. As she is the key to the final portion of my masterpiece, her fame will be all that I need to complete my theorem. Her accomplishment will ensure my success in applying Discordian principles to social processes. She is not strong enough yet, but in the next few weeks, chaos will strengthen and enlighten her while paving the way for her success.

The key, as I fortuitously discovered early in life, was the ability to gain influence over my subjects. That influence was well placed but inert in the social process. Through their trust, I have been given the ability to unleash a chaos of earthly ills upon my subjects' blissful but unconscious lives. Where others have failed, I shall succeed in proving the superior power of chaos, and I shall rise to lead.

Ivy had her own agenda for Lily, and it had started with her mother, Veronica. Ivy had attended the same community college as Veronica, and they became close friends while working toward their degrees. Veronica had gone on to graduate and marry Josh Stanton. His family owned a biotech company where she served as an intern in the marketing department. Eventually, she would work her way up to COO.

Ivy chose to continue her academic career, going on to complete her doctorate in philosophical studies. She began working as a psychic in order to pay for school. A large portion of her studies revolved around religion and spirituality. She then took a particular interest in a new radical religious sect rooted in Discordianism. A small group of students formed a sect called the Eristocrats.

The Discordians worshiped Eris, the Greek goddess of chaos. They believed both order and disorder were merely illusions. Whereas societal structure was built on order, it was a false sense of order that had been structured thousands of years ago by a privileged few that rose to power. Chaos was the true power, and those who accepted chaos were stronger.

The Eristocrats took Discordian principles one step further. They believed the monarchies formed out of Europe and Asia so many thousands of years ago came to power out of chaos. They claimed to be able to trace many of the kings in the early days to a secret society that worshiped Eris as the superior goddess. They called themselves the Eristocrats. This hidden group had helped form organized, orderly societal structures and governments as an illusion. They had led the masses to believe that order was necessary, and chaos was evil. Upon doing so, they had cleverly concealed the power and beauty of chaos so they could maintain their own power, wealth, and status. For those who believed, the true and original Eristocrats were responsible for the very beginnings of governmental structure.

When Ivy discovered this group, she believed she had found the truth that all the world had been built on. She was also led to believe by these religious leaders that her lineage could be traced back to royalty. She worshipped Eris as the one and only true goddess from which all greatness and enlightenment flowed.

Everything made sense to her upon joining the Eristocrats. Her whole life had been built on chaos. She had grown up with a crazy mother who dragged her all over the country following hippie bands and living in different communes with whatever man she was in love with for the moment. Ivy had no formal schooling and no structure. She was self-taught, but in some of the communes, she found mentors who guided her to certain books and spiritual teachings.

By the time she turned eighteen, she was ready for school and all of the structure that came with it. She wanted the order of college life. Ivy was embarrassed by her mother's lifestyle, but she was proud that she was able to manage the chaos in her life on her own. She knew it was chaos that made her strong and independent. She truly believed that only people who could rise out of pure chaos were the strongest and would become the most powerful. Order alone suppressed one's creativity, abilities, and energy until chaos ignited it.

The religion consumed Ivy from the moment she was introduced to the Eristocrats. She recognized her calling. She soon decided to dedicate her life to proving the power of chaos, furthering the Eristocrats, and gaining the power she felt was owed to her. Ivy believed she was to become their queen, the one who would lead the Eristocrats to power and influence over the rest of society.

Her earliest journal entries noted a growing passion for this religious sect, and the beginning of a quest to prove their theories.

Disoriented and somewhat paralyzed by my mother's lifestyle, I was proud that I could transform the energy of such chaos into endless power, and master the order of academia. I recognized that chaos had made me strong and independent, and it is only out of pure chaos that one could be transformed so as to gain power.

People thrive on chaos. It forces them to think faster, adapt more quickly, and stretch their minds to the outer limits. Through chaos, one can gain greater strength and achieve more than those who live by strict regimen and order in their lives.

8

Influence Gained

Soon after becoming friends with Veronica, Ivy started to have her visit for palm readings just for fun while she tried to grow her business. Veronica was on the verge of getting married, but she questioned her decision. She wasn't in love with Josh, but he was very kind and could take care of her. Ivy made her believe her future was with Josh. She must marry him, and they would have two children, and live happily ever after. Veronica married Josh, entered the family business making more money than she had ever imagined, and became more dependent on Ivy for guidance.

Ivy was shocked by the influence she had, and she decided to use Veronica for an experiment. She wanted to prove how powerful she could make Veronica by introducing chaos into her life. Veronica had been raised in a Southern Baptist family with unyielding routine and order based on a strict moral code. Ivy wanted to free her from tradition and elevate her to a position of power within the elitist world of corporate greed.

Veronica had no idea she was being manipulated. She thought Ivy was her only true friend—more like a sister—and she relied on her for support and for assistance in making all of her major decisions. She treated Ivy like a member of her family and encouraged her daughters to think of her as an aunt. She was naïve about Ivy's true intentions and never aware of her involvement with the Eristocrats or her dedication to chaos.

Early on, Ivy documented Veronica's history as a part of the journal that would soon become critical evidence to the Eristocrats.

Veronica will be a key part of proving my theory, even though she's never had any idea I was using her as a subject. I had to demonstrate that a heavy dose of chaos was responsible for Veronica's success. The more chaos that was introduced to her life, the more she achieved. Veronica escaped her rural upbringing and became part of the Stanton family. She was raised in a disciplined, stern family who lived in poverty. She spent most of her childhood merely existing to eat, sleep, pray and go to school. Her father was a preacher in a small town in Mississippi. Her mother was blind and restricted in what she could do. They provided little fun or joy for Veronica and her sister, Hilary. They had no television, no toys, and only library books to keep them entertained. When the girls asked why they didn't have things like the rest of their friends, their father would tell them over and over again that God would provide; that they simply needed to pray harder. But as hard as she prayed, nothing ever changed. She knew as soon as she was old enough, she would get far, far away and never look back.

Veronica's upbringing was a stark contrast to that of her husband, Josh. He never had to want; everything was given to him. As life was so easy, he had little drive or ambition. It's no surprise that he landed in the same community college Veronica attended. She had received a full scholarship from an endowment that helped economically disadvantaged families in the South.

Unlike Veronica, Josh never really wanted to leave home. He stayed in Oak Hill, fell in love with her, and knew that if they were to marry, he could give his parents the grandchildren they desired, and he could easily remain an heir to the estate. He had no interest in the family business, and spent only two years at the company before Veronica gave birth to Ella, later followed by Lily—allowing Josh to stay home and care for them, a role he adored.

9

Accidental Reunion

Lily was driving to the mall, thinking of the perfect green dress, when she felt a jolt. A car had tapped the rear bumper of the Jaguar.

Lily leapt out of the car and saw a tall, slim but muscular man slowly walking toward her from a big old blue Monte Carlo speckled with rust. His tank top revealed tattoos that spanned from his hands to his neck. Lily didn't have tattoos. *Why would anyone do that to his own skin?* She treated her body like a temple. *Why put graffiti on a temple?* She slowed her approach, a little scared as he walked more quickly, black shades hiding his eyes, hair that was merely stubble on the sides and long on the top, a messy faux Mohawk atop his head. Multiple earrings littered his ears, and a simple silver stud pierced the middle of his chin. She kept her hand in her purse. *Oops, no pepper spray today. Just the phone.*

"Hey, Lily, are you OK?" he asked.

She was startled. "I…I'm fine. How, um, how do you know my name?" she fumbled.

He removed his shades. "It's me, Oliver. Remember me? It's been so long, Lily. Uh, sorry about the car." He smiled meekly.

"Oliver, oh my gosh! You look so different. I haven't seen you, I guess, since junior high—since that party at your mom's house…that was so long ago," she exclaimed and gave him a big hug. "I didn't recognize you. Where have you been?" Lily's mother, Veronica, and Oliver's mother, Hilary, were sisters, but they despised each other. Although their families were not close now, they had spent a great deal of time together as children. Oliver and his sister, Sara, were Lily's only two cousins.

"I was just down in Florida this past year, working the clubs as a DJ at night, some construction in the day, but I moved back in February. Hey, I'm really sorry about the car. Can I give you some cash? Not sure if I got caught up with my insurance here yet, but I've got some cash." He removed his wallet from his back pocket while taking a small step back. He knew she wouldn't take his money. Why would she? Her mother had millions. He just wanted to get on his way.

"No, I'm sorry. This was totally my fault. I started to go, and then I saw a squirrel running out in front of me. I guess I should have kept going. Can I help pay for your damage?" She was still stunned that this was Oliver. She thought it was so sad that their mothers hadn't spoken in all these years and couldn't find a way to come together.

"No, no, this car's just a work in progress. No big deal. I gotta get goin' though. So, sure you're good?" he asked, stepping back a little more, inching back to his car.

"Yes, I'm sure I'm fine. So, we should catch up soon. Will I see you around sometime?" Lily thought it might be good to keep in touch. She didn't have contact with much extended family, and it must be fate that they ran into each other like this.

"Yeah, well, I'm working a lot, but I'm sure we'll run into each other soon." His hand was on the Monte Carlo's door handle.

"Oh, OK, I'll pop in sometime, and if you get a chance, you can see me on *American Idol* in a couple of weeks. I just found out I made the show." She could hardly contain her excitement.

"Ah, that's great. I just got a call that I'll be helping on the sound crew. I'm on my way there now to meet with a tech guy on the set," he explained.

"Are you kidding? That's amazing! What are the odds? Well, I'll look for you there!"

Oliver pulled his shades back down over his eyes. "Yeah, I'll be seeing you soon then. I—I gotta run, but good luck on the show."

"Yeah, you too. It's really great to see you!"

Back on the road again, Lily remembered Cole's trial and quickly texted Denny, annoyed that he had gone all day without providing her with an update.

"Where r u? Is the verdict in yet? What happened? CALL me!" she texted.

She didn't really expect him to call, so she checked the local news station's Twitter feed:

"Cole Wells verdict: Not guilty, taken to Community North hospital. Assaulted by his dad, head trauma, now in surgery."

What? That makes no sense, she thought. *Cole was his father's whole life. What did that mean—assault? Something must have been lost in translation.*

10

A Request

Still at the hospital, Ella had just finished her part in the press conference. She briefly announced that her team would keep Cole in a coma until they thought sufficient time had passed for him to heal more safely. Her conversation with Jack had mystified her. She needed further details, but how could she contact him—and what would his next request be?

As the press conference continued, the police answered a few questions about Jack, but they refused to speculate about his motive for hitting his own son. Because of Cole's status as spokesperson with the Special Olympics, the community adored him and wanted to protect him. Their concern for him seemed to intensify after the verdict, which caused most people to believe he had been set up in the drug scandal.

When Ella returned to her office, the phone on her desk was ringing. "Ella, this is Jack again. I just saw you on the news. How is Cole really doing?"

"He actually appears to be doing quite well," she said. "The swelling has already started to recede, and since he's in such great athletic shape, I expect he will heal quite quickly."

"How long will he be in the coma?" Jack asked.

"I believe tomorrow we will be able to start to take him off the medications that induced it."

"No, no! You must leave him in the coma as long as you can—a week at least. His very life depends on it. You've got to trust me. Can you do that?"

"Jack, I'm not the only physician on his case. How can I justify a whole week? I don't know how you expect me to do that. I'll need some kind of support," she insisted.

"I know. It's OK. Find his psychiatrist, Dr. Michaels. He's worked with Cole for years and will back you up on any decision you make. He knows Cole's history. He'll be able to help you."

"But he's just a psychiatrist, how am I supposed to…" Ella heard the dial tone. Jack was gone.

Dr. Michaels had a history not only with Cole, but also with Ella's father. Although Ella knew him on a professional level, he wouldn't discuss much of her father's case with her. She wasn't fond of him. Dr. Michaels had been in some hot water with the hospital administration over allegations of inappropriate contact with female patients. He should have been fired a long time ago, but somehow he was still there.

When her father started unraveling and became unstable last year, Ella had not known of such allegations. She set up his regular appointments with Dr. Michaels. At the time, the family wasn't sure if Josh was losing his mind, just depressed, or beginning to experience dementia. He had been raising some chickens and a cow, essentially farming about an acre of the family estate while residing in a small unkempt pool house. He refused to be part of any family function unless it took place at his "farm." As Josh became more and more unreasonable, Ella decided Dr. Michaels wasn't doing his job, especially since he didn't share his conclusions with her. Josh seemed to be on the decline and kept his appointments only once every few months.

Ella was no fan of Dr. Michaels, but she had to ask for his help. He would probably think she was crazy if she asked him to help justify keeping Cole in a coma. She went to his office immediately, but the receptionist told her he was on leave for the rest of the week. She handed Ella a note from him. *How did Dr. Michaels know I'd be coming to see him? How could he possibly know Cole's secrets?*

11

A Proposal

Ella headed to the cafeteria. She was famished, and she couldn't wait to sit down and read the note from Dr. Michaels. On her way, she ran into Denny in the hallway. He had been at the hospital for the press conference and was looking for Ella to help him make an important decision.

"Hi, Ella. Could I talk to you for a minute—privately?" he asked nervously.

"Sure, what's up? This isn't about Cole, is it? You know I can't tell you anything I wouldn't tell the rest of the press."

"Oh, no, of course not. I wouldn't ask you to do that. I just take the video, you know?" he grinned widely.

"OK, let's go to my office then," she said, hoping this would be quick.

As she sat at her desk, Denny pulled a box out of his pocket and opened it to display a diamond ring, a smallish oval gem, maybe a carat, set in platinum. "I want to ask Lily to marry me, but I don't know if I should ask your dad first. What do you think? Will she like this ring? Do you think she'll be surprised? I can't wait to ask her. I don't have a plan yet, but it'll come to me."

Ella was stunned. Denny had been with Lily for over a year, but they were so young. She felt a little sad for a moment. Although she was six years older than Lily, she had never had a serious relationship, let alone a marriage proposal. Sometimes, she felt she would never find anyone.

"That's fantastic, and the ring—it's beautiful! I know Lily will be so excited. I wouldn't go to Dad. He hasn't been himself lately, so it would be best not to bother him. He hasn't been taking his meds; his behavior is just too unpredictable right now. Lily can tell him in her own way, later on. It will be just fine," she said.

Denny felt better and gave Ella a big hug. He couldn't wait to pop the question to Lily. As he left, Ella shut the door behind him and locked it. She didn't want to be interrupted as she read the note from Dr. Michaels.

Ella, Attached is a letter of support for your decision to allow Cole to remain in a coma. Don't worry—just keep things on a day-to-day basis and no one will challenge you on this matter.

See you soon,

Dr. Michaels

That was it? Well, that was easy, Ella thought to herself. *How did he already know I needed his support? What does he know about Cole and his dad?* Ella expected that with his support, she wouldn't encounter any other opposition to her treatment decisions for Cole. She was well-respected in this county hospital that was understaffed and struggling to keep up with the revolving door of patients. Though she couldn't help but wonder if she should just tell the police about her conversation with Jack.

As she puzzled about where she might find Dr. Michaels, the phone rang. It was her mother. Veronica shouted, "Ella, I need you to get over to that damn farm right away! I can't find Lily, and your father is up in a tree and won't come down. He says that he needs to be one with nature. What in the world does that mean? I don't have time for this. Please tell me you're available!"

"Yes, of course, I'm leaving the hospital now. I'll talk to you later." Ella sighed as she put her phone away and grabbed her things.

Veronica had been under enormous pressure from representatives of the Department of Justice. They were investigating allegations of off-label promotion of her company's newest biologic agent to physicians. They alleged that drug reps had been talking to doctors about what the agent could do for breast cancer patients, but it had been approved for only leukemia patients. It would mean a hefty fine from the government if they could prove their case. For Veronica, it meant many hours with attorneys prepping for the hearing.

Since it was near the end of the day, there was nothing more to be done for Cole until tomorrow. Then, Ella would have to update his status and provide a rationale for keeping him in a coma. Her mother could care less about Josh and would probably be happy for him to stay up in the tree. She just didn't want the public embarrassment of being married to a mad man. Ella loved her father, but she dreaded spending time with her mother.

12

Progress Update

I vy periodically sent updates as to the status of her experiment to the Eristocrats. She planned to use that information as a basis for proving the theory of their religion.

A SUMMARY OF RECENT DEVELOPMENTS:

I have designed an approach that may be the key to the application of Discordian theory, an area from which the majority of my academic colleagues seem disengaged.

It is true that the only way to peace and enlightenment is to embrace the chaos around us and harness its strength for the good of mankind. To prove this theory, it is also true that the ends justify the means. Thus, I will organize my activity into easily understandable case studies that will help provide greater credibility for the good of the religion.

I need to demonstrate the efficacy of the technique of using chaos to achieve the goals for subjects in five areas:

- INFLUENCE
- WEALTH
- POWER
- LOVE
- FAME

I have achieved all of these goals and am currently working to shape the last one, which is FAME for Miss Lily Stanton.

INFLUENCE was the area in which I served as my own subject, not only by struggling to emerge from the quagmire of my mother's life and using the released energy to develop a work process, but especially by stumbling upon what initially seemed to me an adolescent game: palmistry. This fortunate discovery placed me in the position of advising others, and the impact was amazing and profound.

Palmistry activated empathy and powerful intuition in me, as well as a right-brain ability to easily absorb the sister arts of astrology, numerology, and more. Combined with my achievement of releasing Veronica into WEALTH, I gained unimagined access to an elite circle, a devoted clientele who regarded me as an important director of their affairs. The point is that once chaos ensues, you will see all kinds of new possibilities for growth in the area that you are activating.

As I have previously written, Veronica helped me complete the case of WEALTH in this study. She came from poverty and now has millions and enough stock in the company to remain a millionaire for the rest of her life. Even her children—and someday, their children—will carry on this wealth. She never could have attained this within the strict, disciplined life she knew as a child. God could not provide her this wealth. It was, of course, Eris, the goddess of chaos, who was responsible for bringing her strength, confidence, and this great fortune.

I now turn to the next phases, which are POWER and LOVE. I have successfully maneuvered a man who was well on his way to becoming a priest into becoming a politician. I conjured up enough chaos in his life to completely transform him into a power-hungry political candidate. I expect him to become a congressman and to eventually work his way up to the senate. Further details of this accomplishment will be detailed in the full dissertation.

LOVE is a most ephemeral area. This was the easiest one to develop because love comes from chaos—think of Cupid's random arrow. There is no rhyme or reason as to how or why two people fall in love and live happily ever after—or not. Even if they fell in love, got married, changed their minds, maybe came together in love for a short period of time, or a long period of time…it doesn't matter. Every person in the world falls in love. The only exceptions I can think of are those in arranged marriages, and even those people often fall in love at least for a moment in time. I have successfully thrown an abundance of clients into relationships, thanks to chaos. Multiple case studies will be detailed in the full dissertation.

The present case is a study of FAME. This is where Lily Stanton comes in. I think that, as a talented singer, Lily is well on her way to fame through the nationally televised competition that is coming up in just a couple of weeks. Through my interference, she will soon find herself in chaos, which, given the timing, I will have to conjure up quickly. It will take some immediate effort to provide enough evidence that would show how she rose to fame, not due to her comfy little world but from the chaos that would, in the end, make her stronger and extraordinarily famous. However, chaos is not something that would find Lily naturally, so I will need to create multiple sources of turmoil around her and force her to react. Lily will require all of my focus and concentration now.

13

A Body in the Night

With Ella on her way to help her father at the estate, Veronica felt free to visit her friend Ivy. She needed some clarity on business issues, and Ivy had always helped her. Veronica was relieved that Ella was always there for her father. She was fed up with Josh. She couldn't divorce him because the corporation was his family's business. She still couldn't believe she found the company far more compelling than he did. She had climbed the corporate ladder while he took care of their home and their children, a satisfying arrangement for both, although they had grown far apart.

When Veronica parked the car, she noticed an ambulance in the front of Ivy's house. She climbed the stairs to the house, an old Victorian structure that sat atop a steep hill. It featured a huge, dimly lit front porch that was particularly eerie at night. As she got closer, the eeriness became ghastly. She could see paramedics placing a white sheet over a body. Fearing something must have happened to Ivy, Veronica ran up the rest of steps to find Denny at the house with camera in hand.

She grabbed him. "Denny, what's going on here? Is it Ivy? It can't be—it can't be. Please, no! Tell me who it is." She shook him.

"Take it easy, Mrs. Stanton. Ivy isn't home. This is some dude Lily found dead on the porch. She came here to show Ivy the dress she picked out for the show and found him on the porch covered in blood. Weird, huh? She freaked out and called me. I came as fast as I could, but by the time I got here, the police had her. They said she had to go in for questioning."

"Why didn't you go with her? She must be scared to death. She's never seen a dead body." Poor Lily. She had no experience with the ugly, dirty things in life. She lived in a safe, extremely comfortable world. She was a sensitive child and certainly not streetwise.

"I tried, but they said I couldn't go. I called this attorney I know, and he told her not to answer questions until he got to the station. I was just trying to get a little footage, and I was hoping to catch Ivy to tell her what happened," he explained. "Lily said Ivy went to the market, and she was going to just wait on the porch until she got back. She must have dropped the dress when she saw the body. I found it. It's in my car."

Veronica rolled her eyes. *What a hero…he saved the dress. Lily shouldn't be at the police station by herself with some second-rate attorney.* "Stay here and wait for Ivy. I'll get our family attorney down there immediately." She was dialing the phone as she barked the order and rushed back to her car.

As the ambulance pulled away, no longer flashing its lights, Ivy rounded the corner down the block with her bag from the market filled with fruit, bread, and an assortment of herbal teas. She had left her phone at home on purpose. She knew what was happening, and she took her time.

After Lily called to tell Ivy she would be coming over to show her the green dress she had chosen, Ivy prepared for chaos to ensue. She had gone out earlier in the afternoon equipped with a bottle of vodka laced with enough cyanide to kill an elephant and slowly cruised Oak Hill's slums until she arrived at a bridge under which several homeless people lived. There, she easily tempted a tooth-less, deranged old man with a love of alcohol. The poor man guzzled the bottle so quickly, he never had a chance. No one else was anywhere in sight. No one would miss him, and no one would look for him. If he couldn't do anything with his life on this earth, then certainly, the afterlife would be a better option. In Ivy's mind, she was merely putting him out of his misery.

She loaded the body into a large garbage container with wheels on the bottom so she could push him to her SUV and unload him into the vehicle. He was a scrawny, little man that she easily rolled into a plastic bag to protect her clothing and then into the vehicle. She quickly drove home and waited for Lily's text. As the sun went down, she unloaded some other garden equipment, mulch and flowers before pulling him from the vehicle and wheeling him up her driveway onto the front porch. This would all appear as a part of her gardening in case anyone was watching. She had a blanket over him and pulled him out onto the porch for Lily to discover. Ivy then removed the blanket, threw some cow's blood on him for a more dramatic effect, and walked down the street toward the store. Next, she texted Lily to say that she was at the market and asked her to wait on the porch.

Lily was horrified when she saw the bloody dead man. She was further traumatized by the police loading her into a car and demanding she come in for questioning. She wasn't under arrest, but she couldn't help thinking she was a murder suspect. She had never been so scared.

14

At the Police Station

Lily walked into the interrogation room, shaking and sobbing. A handsome blond, fit man wearing a prim shirt and tie was standing in the corner. He told her to take a seat, and his kind eyes immediately got her attention.

"Relax. There's no need for crying. We know you had nothing to do with this man's death. That's not really why you're here. From all appearances, it looks like a vagrant wandered onto the porch and likely died of an overdose or natural causes. We're not sure about the blood since there were no apparent external injuries but it's not important. We wanted to bring you in for questioning to cover all bases but mostly we want to know more about the homeowner. I need a little bit more information if you're willing to help us," he said. "I'm Detective Matthews, by the way." He smiled and called for someone to bring her a bottle of water and a box of tissues.

Lily nodded. "OK. I don't know anything much, I really don't. But, yes, of course, I want to help if I can," Lily said as she sniffled and blew into a tissue one of the policemen had given her.

"Thank you. What I'd like to know is a little more about Ms. Ivy Keller, and your relationship with her. Have you known her long?" he asked slowly. "And just how do you know her?"

"She's my advisor. Sometimes she reads my palm or tarot cards or just advises me on things I should do or what direction to take. She's more than psychic.

She knows about everything—spiritual things, astrology, and more. Plus, she's my mom's best friend. She's like an aunt to me; like part of our family. She helps me with everything important." As Lily spoke, she felt confused.

"Has she ever tried to get you to join a religious group or anything like that?" the detective asked while taking notes.

"No, I don't know about any religious group, and she's not like that. She doesn't go to church or anything or talk about God at all. Why do you ask?"

"We just want to get a better idea of her character so we can rule her out as a suspect," Matthews replied. Actually, he had been looking into the Eristocrat group and believed Ivy and this group may be highly dangerous. "Has she ever tried to sell you drugs or given you drugs of any kind?"

"No way! I would never do drugs and neither would Ivy. She hardly even drinks at all!"

"What about any boyfriends? Is she dating or close to anyone that you know of?"

"No, there used to be a guy she was kind of dating four or five years ago, but I don't think she's been with anyone since," Lily said as she wondered what had happened to him. She would never know, for Ivy was extremely private about her social life and anything personal.

Just then, the door flew open. Veronica Stanton grabbed her daughter by the shoulder. "Lily, why are you talking to this policeman by yourself? Come with me, now," she demanded, pulling her out of the chair.

"Ma'am, you can't just barge in here like this!" Matthews exclaimed.

"And you can't just question my daughter like this, without counsel!" Veronica was beyond angry.

"Mom, it's OK. He knows I didn't do anything to that man, and we were just talking," Lily said, trying to calm her mother down.

"I don't care—this is unacceptable. You can speak to our attorney if you need something, but don't you dare upset my daughter any further," she said as she pulled Lily by the hand and promptly left the station.

As Veronica drove her daughter to the estate, she called Denny at Ivy's where she had left him to update her friend. He told her Ivy was upset and concerned. "So are we all," Veronica replied grimly and instructed him to join them at the estate.

As Veronica pulled into the estate, she drove past the pool house where the lights were on. Ella's car was in front with another car that she didn't recognize. Ella must have gotten her father out of the tree, but Veronica couldn't guess who else would be there with her. She decided she would wait at the main house until Denny arrived and then go back to the pool house to check.

15

Old Affairs

Ella had been able to calm her father down. Josh had been acting like a monkey. He was screeching and trying to swing from the tree branches. She was able to reach Dr. Michaels on his cell. Despite his being on leave from the hospital, he agreed to help immediately. He sedated Josh and got him back to bed in the pool house. Even though she wasn't fond of Dr. Michaels, Ella was now quite grateful for his help. She was also curious about his leave from the hospital and why he thought it was necessary and safe to put Cole in a coma for a week.

With a freshly opened bottle of wine on hand, Ella sat with Dr. Michaels at the card table in the main room of the pool house. As a collector of fine red wines, Josh had stocked the cabinets with enough bottles to last a decade. As they discussed next steps, he told her that he had taken a vial of Josh's blood and was going to run some tests. He noted that her dad hadn't seen his regular family doctor for years, nor had any other professional run his bloodwork. Dr. Michaels suspected dementia. Ella felt better. Dr. Michaels at least cared about her dad even if he seemed kind of shady. Still, she wondered about his treatment of Cole.

"So why are you away from the hospital? Is this a vacation, or are you working on something?" she asked.

"I have some business to take care of, and I just need some time," he said before sipping his wine.

"So, what about Cole? How did you know I would be asking you for help, and why does he need to stay in a coma for so long?" Just then, Veronica entered swiftly.

"Well, isn't this cozy?" She was surprised to see Dr. Michaels with her daughter. "I assume Dr. Michaels is here helping your father." Veronica had been very careful not to get caught in the affair she had had with him a couple of years ago. It had ended quite badly when she found him with another woman. Ella had no idea about the affair but knew her mother was no fan of her father's psychiatrist.

"Yes, well, we got him out of the tree, and he's sleeping in the other room now."

"We'll be running some tests to see if something else is going on with him," Dr. Michaels added a bit nervously. Veronica always intimidated him.

"Tests, what tests? He just needs to go to his appointments regularly, but neither of you seem to be able to hold him accountable for that or help make sure he shows up—or even bother to let me know when he doesn't. Ella, you can go home now—or better yet, go up to the house and visit your sister. Lily's day has been a nightmare. I want to speak to Dr. Michaels privately," she ordered.

Ella was happy to leave rather than listen to her mother's tirade. She wanted answers to more questions about Cole but definitely couldn't talk about it with her mother there. "Dr. Michaels, I would like to see you at the hospital after you've done the blood tests."

As Ella exited, she realized one of the windows was open, and she could hear everything her mother was saying. Hidden from their view, she decided to listen for a moment.

"Dr. Michaels, you are not leaving this property with my husband's blood. You did not have permission to take it, and I will call the police to report you right now," she said, holding her cell phone in one hand and a broomstick in the other.

Dr. Michaels knew her actions were purely spiteful. She would like him to have nothing to do with their family. "Fine, here it is then." He pulled the vial of blood from his pocket and placed it on the table. He thought perhaps she just needed a little attention and affection. Then, he walked over to Veronica, put his arms around her, and started to stroke her hair. She pulled the broomstick up and whacked him in the back of the head several times as Dr. Michaels tried to duck and squealed in pain.

"What are you doing? Put the broom down! Have you lost your mind?" he screamed while holding his head.

Veronica threw the broom down and dismissed him as she pointed to the door. "Out, get out now!" she said, seething with anger.

Ella was startled. She hadn't seen Dr. Michaels's attempt at affection, but she heard the attack and thought her mother had struck him for no reason. She left abruptly and walked toward the house.

When Ella got to the house, she entered the family room, thinking she'd say a quick hello to Lily and Denny before Veronica got back. The family room was dark except for the glow of the fireplace, and she could see them sitting on the floor by the fire with Lily crying on Denny's shoulder.

"Lily, what's wrong?" Ella asked as she entered the room.

Lily and Denny looked up startled. Then, she smiled and held up her left hand to show a new diamond on her ring finger. "Denny proposed! We're getting married!" she exclaimed with tears still streaming down her face.

Ella congratulated them. Then, Lily caught her up on the story about the dead man and her adventures at the police station. While they were talking, Veronica returned through the back of the house and went up the stairs to her bedroom without saying a word to anyone. She took the blood, emptied it into the sink, and threw away the vial. She was furious about her encounter with Dr. Michaels and the fact that he was on her property at all.

Later, realizing how late it had become, Ella suddenly couldn't wait to get home and get some rest. As she neared her car in front of the pool house, where her dad was still sleeping off the sedatives, Dr. Michaels suddenly crept out of the bushes toward her. He had parked his car at the front of the gate and walked back in order to catch Ella before she left. He wanted to help her dad and knew his condition was getting worse. Veronica wasn't helping the situation.

"Ella, I was waiting for you. I don't understand why your mother won't allow the blood tests, but we need to see if there is something more to his condition— some underlying problem we need to figure out. Can you try to take some blood and work with the lab on getting those tests ordered?"

"Yes, of course. I'll take it while he's still sleeping before I leave," she said as her thoughts jumped ahead to Cole. Maybe he would give her more information. "Can you tell me more about Cole, though? Why do we need to leave him in a coma for a full week? Have you been in contact with his dad? What are we waiting for?"

"I know you want more information, but I can't tell you very much. You know about the drug charges. Well, there are some people he dealt with who would rather he went to prison or that he didn't come out of the coma at all. His dad is going to try to fix things and just needs some time. Cole is safe if he's in a coma and can't talk. That's really all I can tell you."

"But Cole was found not guilty. He was surely just taken advantage of and used. He didn't know he was delivering drugs, and he isn't capable of being in some kind of big drug business."

"That's not exactly true. It seems he was actually quite involved in the drug business and may have been pretty high in the chain of command. I can't tell you any more than that, and you need to stay quiet about all of this, or your life could be in danger too. I'll be in touch about Cole, but, in the meantime, get your father's bloodwork done, and we'll see what it shows."

16

Old Photos

I vy shared some pastries and coffee with Veronica at Ivy's house the next morning before heading to the office. They chatted for nearly an hour. Ivy seemed calm and nearly unconcerned about the dead man, but when Veronica told her about Josh and the encounter with Dr. Michaels, Ivy insisted that she stay far away from him. Ivy knew he could cause great damage to her own future plans.

That morning, still at the estate, a shocked Lily sat on her bed in her room sorting through photos she had discovered in an envelope on her dresser. The pictures showed her mother kissing Dr. Michaels. Next, they were undressing each other, both nude and romping on a hotel bed. Then, it got worse. She didn't want to look, but she forced herself to gather more information. Several liaisons occurred. Eight occasions, dated about two years ago, occurring in different locations: hotels, an office, or at the hospital, she couldn't tell from the setting. The heated, erotic scenes were graphic and clearly not meant to be caught on film. Lily was horrified, angry, hurt, and so nauseated that she gagged. With tears of rage and sorrow in her eyes, she threw the photos away from her.

When she had calmed, Lily stuffed the photos back into the envelope just to get them out of sight. Why were they in her room? This was no accident. She suddenly felt unsafe in her own surroundings. Clearly someone had entered her room and left the pictures there for her.

Lily was well aware that her mother wasn't in love with her father, but she never thought she would do this. Her mother was such a respectable businesswoman. How could she carry on with her own husband's psychiatrist, and was the affair still going on?

Lily felt as if for every good thing that happened, something awful would happen. The past week had been full of so many highs and so many lows. Making the cut for *American Idol* and Denny's proposal had made her so happy, but, on the opposite end of the spectrum, she had found that ghastly scene with the dead man, and now, her mother wasn't at all the person Lily believed she was.

She was angry and wanted to move out of the house that instant. Denny had been asking her to move into his apartment. Now that they were engaged, it just made sense. If she were to move though, she needed to make sure her dad would be all right. For the most part, she knew he was well taken care of, as the estate caretakers loved him and made sure he had everything he desired in the pool house where he'd been staying for several years now. He had a cook who brought him all of his meals. He spent his days gardening and caring for his animals.

Lily phoned her sister as she packed her clothes and Ella explained how she had taken blood from their father and then the shocking results. Ella had discovered that his blood contained small amounts of ethylene glycol—antifreeze—in his blood. He had either ingested accidentally, or someone was poisoning him. The amount wasn't enough to be fatal, but it was enough to sicken him physically and mentally. It was hard to tell how long this had been going on, but it certainly explained his strange behavior over the past year.

After that news, Lily decided not to tell Ella about the photos. Although she feared the poisoning might implicate her mother, or even Dr. Michaels, it was too soon to leap to conclusions. It would be better to confront her mother alone first.

17

Mansion of Mystery

Ella had scheduled their father to be hospitalized for a detox treatment, which would hopefully help bring him back to normal again. Lily would need to bring him into the hospital without alarming anyone. She would also need to figure out how to tell her mother about the tests and that she had taken his blood. The police would have to perform a thorough investigation of the family, the staff, and all acquaintances. They didn't want anyone at the estate to know what Ella had discovered about Josh's poisoning. Everyone would have to be treated like a suspect. Ella hoped it wouldn't take too long to figure out who was responsible. She couldn't imagine who would do such a thing. She still couldn't believe someone would be out to kill or hurt her father. Maybe the poisoning was accidental. Josh had been around so many chemicals while he was gardening. There just had to be a rational explanation for it.

As Ella thought through all of the possibilities, she received a call from Dr. Michaels. She was anxious to tell him about the tests and get his opinion. After her report, he asked her to meet him. He had recommendations about her father's treatment, along with some information about Cole.

Upon getting her father settled in the hospital, Ella met Dr. Michaels that afternoon at the address he had given her. It was a luxurious, stunning house in the historic district of downtown Oak Hill. On the outside, it was a beautiful brick and limestone home from the 1800s, but the interior had been completely transformed into a modern, ultra-chic space with exquisite furnishings and décor. Such a house could not belong to Dr. Michaels. As a psychiatrist, he had a good income, but this palatial property was beyond his means and certainly beyond his taste.

"Wow, this place is gorgeous!" Ella exclaimed as she wandered from the living room into the kitchen, paying close attention to the expensive art pieces on the walls. "Who lives here? It's so beautiful."

"Yes, I wanted you to meet me here because you have to see it to believe it. I know you'll think this is crazy, but it appears this is actually Cole's house," he said as he opened the refrigerator and searched for something to drink.

"Wait, what? Cole—who's in a coma—that Cole? That's impossible. He lives near the community center in a small apartment that Jack rented for him. During the trial, it was all over the news."

"Well, somehow Jack figured out just a few weeks ago that this is his real home. As his father, he wasn't allowed to be part of the official investigation, but he wanted to prove that Cole was innocent. He did his own investigating and found this place," he explained as he looked through a mostly empty fridge. "He doesn't know who set him up in this house or how that person managed to do so. What he does know is that his son is heavily involved in dealing drugs. Jack gave me the key to this place to look around and keep an eye open for criminal activity that might be going on here."

"So, where is Jack? And what happened at the courthouse?"

"Well it seems Jack had just figured out that Cole had been living a double life. He was livid! He felt betrayed and was overcome by anger. He told me he watched Cole walk out of the courthouse with a wink, like he knew he had gotten away with something. His dad lives by the rules and the law. Cole somehow got messed up in something big. Jack loves his son, of course, but Cole put his own father's career and his reputation in jeopardy, and he lied to his father for a long time. Jack just snapped. He couldn't help it, and now he feels awful and is trying to help save his son from somebody who seems to want him dead," he explained while munching on a slice of cheese. "Right now, he's in California checking on a lead. He doesn't know who wants to kill Cole, but it must have something to do with a deal gone bad. That's why he needs some time to figure out the details."

"But what if he needs more than just a week?" Ella wondered if it was really worth compromising her ethics and profession to save a drug dealer. Even if he was mentally challenged and someone had probably taken advantage of him, Cole certainly had enough sense to know right from wrong.

"Well, we'll just see what happens. We can only do what we can do," he said.

"You'll have to find out soon if Jack's making progress. We only have four more days to keep him in the coma."

"Yes, I'll be speaking with Jack this evening and should get more information."

"Dr. Michaels, I need your help with my dad too. I told you about the blood tests, and I need you to help him understand what's happened. You're his psychiatrist; he's going to need you. He'll stay with me once he's out of the hospital. He can't go back to the estate while they're investigating the staff."

"Of course, I'm happy to help. We should have dinner tonight, and we can put together a plan," he said putting his hand on her shoulder and thinking that even though Ella was much younger, she might be interested in him for something more.

Ella was fairly naïve when it came to men. She hadn't had much experience dating and didn't think of herself as very attractive. She knew he had a reputation for being a womanizer, but it didn't even occur to her that Dr. Michaels would think of her as anything other than a colleague.

Ella was still amazed by the house. She wanted to look around some more, so she suggested they meet back again for dinner. She would cook dinner, and they could look for clues that might help Jack.

Ella went to the store for a few things to make a simple dinner. Her father was safe at the hospital for the next few days, and she didn't need to be there until morning. She left a message for her mother explaining that she had admitted Josh to the hospital for some mental tests and to watch his behavior. She gave no indication of the blood test or the poisoning. It was better not to alarm her over the phone. She did not yet know that her sister had discovered the photos and was moving in with Denny. She thought Lily could break the news and explain the situation to their mother back at the estate.

As Ella waited for the lasagna to finish cooking, she began searching the house, looking in each of the five bedrooms, the bathrooms, the basement, and all of the many closets. There were hardly any personal items other than a few articles of clothing in the closet and dresser of the master bedroom, some bathroom toiletries, and a couple of towels. The kitchen was virtually empty as well. Ella thought maybe someone had come through months ago when he first went to jail and cleaned the place of anything in case the police discovered it.

The only thing she found that was strange was a tiny baby sock mixed in with a few men's socks in a dresser drawer. She didn't know what to make of it, if anything, but she took the tiny sock and stuck it in her pocket.

18

Miscommunications

Having received Ella's message, Veronica prepared to go to the hospital to speak with the doctors and visit her husband. When she went to her room to change, she discovered that Lily had left a sealed envelope on her bed. There was a note on the outside:

Mom, I don't know where these pictures came from, but someone left them in my room. I'm moving in with Denny. I'll get the rest of my things later, please don't call me.

Lily

Veronica flipped through the photos with disgust and seething rage. Who had done this? The affair was over two years ago, so why was it coming to the surface now? If someone wanted money, she would surely have heard by now. Maybe her lover (she shuddered) took the photos himself and was toying with her. Maybe Lily inadvertently received them instead of her—or maybe the government investigators who were looking into the biotech company had started to look at her personal life. Then again, why would they care? She didn't have answers, but she vowed to find them and soon.

Veronica went into Lily's room to find most of the clothes gone from the closet, along with her jewelry and all of her makeup. Some things were strewn about the room haphazardly, but among the shoes on the closet floor, there was a bag from the *American Idol* show. Veronica opened the bag to find some products that the show's producers were likely giving to all the performers. All of the items featured the show's logo. There was a T-shirt, a coffee mug, some pens, and even an iPad. As she removed the items, she found a bag of marijuana and a small bag containing several pills. She never suspected either of her daughters of engaging in any sort of drug activity and was astonished that little Lily would have the nerve to bring them into her mother's home.

She grabbed the drugs and went back to her own room to dispose of them, along with the photos. First, she tossed the photos into the fireplace. As they curled into ash, she heard a knock at the door. She threw the drugs in her purse and answered the door. The caretaker informed her that police investigators had arrived with a search warrant. He filled her in on the stated reasons for the search and the alleged poisoning of her husband. All day long, both of her daughters had failed to mention any of this, and now, the entire estate was going to be torn apart by police officers. Her heart raced as she realized what was happening.

Veronica was now boiling over with rage. The investigators were on the first floor looking through everything. They took items of interest and seemed to dismantle everything they touched. Veronica called Lily. There was no answer, so she left an angry message demanding that she come home that instant to tell her where and how she got those photos. She screamed into the phone and was loud enough for all of the policeman on the property to hear her. "And Lily, you need to get here now. The police are going through everything in the house, including your room so they're going to want to question you about some things. I'm with the lead investigator right now, and he wants to talk to you specifically. You'll need to be here for them immediately. They want answers from you. You need to answer for what you've done!" She wanted to scare Lily since she had the nerve to bring drugs into her house. If the investigators found them in her purse, she wouldn't hesitate to turn Lily in to them. Veronica even thought for a moment about turning them over to the police anyway, but she changed her mind and flushed it all down the toilet. She would deal with Lily herself.

This disaster would surely be in the news before tomorrow morning if it hadn't already been posted somewhere. Veronica didn't need any more bad publicity. She'd had enough from the company investigation, and soon, everyone would be wondering if she had tried to kill her husband.

As Lily listened with some fear to her mother's rant on her voicemail, she wondered what she meant. *Question me about what? That didn't make any sense.* Lily had never had anything to hide from the police. She couldn't possibly think that Lily could poison her own father but maybe she was instead worried about herself. The police would certainly suspect Veronica. The spouse is always a suspect in these situations. Perhaps, she was trying to divert their suspicions to Lily? Her mother may in fact be trying to frame her for her father's poisoning. Now that Lily knew about the affair, Veronica must have realized that she had discovered a motive for the poisoning.

Lily's mind was spinning out of control with crazed thoughts. She didn't know anything about her grandparents' will or who would inherit the estate, the business, and all of the assets once they passed, but she assumed her mother would inherit everything if her father were deceased or declared mentally incompetent. She wouldn't inherit anything if Lily went to the police about the photos and her suspicions. Her mother was extremely smart, and Lily thought she was probably planting the evidence right now so she would take the fall. Lily started to panic. Her head was reeling. Everything she thought of threw her life into greater discord. She felt as if she were going mad.

Lily had no knowledge of the drugs that were in her bag. They ended up there on the occasion of one of the rehearsals inadvertently from her cousin, Oliver. He had been hired as a sound technician for the show, and everyone received the same bag from *American Idol* as a promotional gift. She had mistakenly picked up Oliver's bag when she left. Earlier, Oliver, who occasionally delivered drugs to make extra money, had stashed his next customer's order in the bag.

Lily's bag contained her wallet with her credits cards and ID. Back at the estate, she had thrown the bag in a corner without realizing she was missing her wallet. She had been at the studio all day for meetings and rehearsals for the show, which would appear on TV in less than two weeks. Already exhausted, she began to reach out to everyone she knew so they would watch and vote for her on the day of the show. She was sending e-mails, tweeting, and posting messages everywhere to appeal to her friends and relatives across the country. She had even mailed decorative handwritten cards to some of her family's friends and business contacts.

Her best rehearsals had taken place that week. Her voice was clear and strong. With all of the craziness that was happening around her, she was able to channel her energy and use singing as an outlet for her stress. When she sang, it all went away, and her focus was on only the sound coming out of her mouth. Her whole body released the tension. It was the best she had ever sounded and the most confident she had felt about her singing.

Still confused by her mother's message, Lily drove straight to Denny's apartment. As she pulled up to his place, she realized she had forgotten her wallet. Lily was certain her mother wouldn't hesitate to set someone up, even her own daughter, if she were in enough trouble. Over time, Veronica had developed into a fighter and a survivor. She cared for her daughters, but ultimately, Veronica's own needs would always come first. While she worked, nannies, along with the estate's caretakers, nurtured Lily and Ella. Those around her considered her to be quite cold and calculating, but these were the qualities that helped her go far in the family business. The only person Veronica was close to was Ivy. Lily knew this well and thought maybe she should talk to Ivy to see what she knew about her mother's motives. Ivy would have some insight into what Lily should do next without her saying anything about her suspicions of Veronica. She decided she wouldn't tell Ivy everything, but perhaps she could reveal just enough to trigger the woman's keen intuition. Ivy may not have been truly psychic, but she could sense much of what was going on with those who were close to her. Maybe her mother had even confided her plans for her father and for her future. Lily knew she needed help. She was exhausted, confused, and in need of direction. She had to take a chance and get some advice from Ivy.

19

Correcting Chaos

Ivy wasn't surprised to see Lily. She knew Lily was distressed from the events of the week. She was happy Lily still sought her advice. She explained how her father was in the hospital and then started crying.

"Lily, my little Lily, you are practically frantic. Your father will be just fine if he is in the hospital now. What is really the matter? You are shaking. Why are you so terrified?"

Lily began sobbing uncontrollably. She couldn't help it. She had to tell Ivy what she suspected about her mother and that she was sure her mother was setting it up to make it look like Lily was responsible for the poisoning. Everything came pouring out. This time, Ivy was stunned. This was not a part of the plan—not at all a part of the plan.

Ivy had been slowly poisoning Lily's father over the past year. She didn't give him enough of the chemical to kill him—not enough to require detoxification. She administered just enough to make him a little bit ill. She wanted to force Veronica to make some decisions about her marriage and her family amid the chaos of Josh's unpredictable and erratic behavior. It was the final part of her plan for Veronica, but no one other than Veronica and Josh were to be involved in this part.

Ivy had been meticulously injecting a precise amount of antifreeze into just one Gatorade bottle out of a six-pack. Josh always had one in the refrigerator at the pool house. Small amounts were undetectable by smell or taste and matched the shade of a green Gatorade. When she visited Veronica at the estate, she would stop there on her way out and leave another pack of Gatorade. Josh was always gardening and drank at least two bottles a day. He received a poisoned drink only once a week at most. No one was to ever find out, and she had planned to stop at the end of the year.

Now, all of her plans were vulnerable, and Lily could be in more danger than she ever imagined—danger that had nothing to do with the possibility that her own mother was setting her up to be accused of her father's poisoning. If Ivy's plans failed, Lily's life would be at risk. She could fall victim to chaos that would spread far beyond Ivy's reach.

Ivy convinced Lily to stay at her house. She slipped a sedative into her hot cocoa, and Lily was fast asleep shortly before sundown. Ivy had to visit Veronica to clear up this confusion. Since neither Veronica nor Lily had been poisoning Josh, Ivy had to find out why Veronica had scared her daughter with threats of police questioning. Perhaps she was just angry over the photos, but she couldn't blame Lily for that. Ivy had to keep Veronica and Lily from destroying each other. A little chaos went a long way at times.

As Ivy drove onto the estate's grounds, the last of the police cars were leaving. Ivy found Veronica cleaning up after they had turned everything inside out. As they discussed what had happened with the police, Ivy reported her conversation with Lily and explained how distraught and confused she was over her mother's rage. Ivy carefully explained why Lily thought Veronica had poisoned Josh.

"Well, of course she thinks I did it. Everyone is going to think that. The police, the news, the staff here—they're all looking at me like I tried to kill my own husband. Just because I'm not in love with him, that doesn't mean I want him dead. There's a big difference! I don't inherit all of this anyway. Though they don't know yet, but Lily and Ella are the ones who get it all. I have nothing to gain."

"Yes, I know, dear," Ivy sympathized, "but why the angry message to Lily about the police? You frightened her terribly."

"Good, she should be scared. She drops off these awful photos of me from two years ago with no explanation, moves in with that moron Denny, and has the nerve to bring drugs into this house, my house! I found a bag of marijuana and pills in her room. I had half a mind to just give it to the police and let her suffer the consequences."

Ivy was annoyed. "Veronica, you know better than that. You protect your own flesh and blood, and you deal with your problems directly. That affair was your mistake, and you can't think she had anything to do with some photos that suddenly popped up. Think before you lose your head. Reacting through emotions is not acceptable. Lily isn't on drugs, and you would know that if you stopped and centered yourself as I have taught you over and over and over again. What is so difficult to understand about that? Center yourself!"

Veronica hung her head. "I know," she said quietly. "I haven't been myself. I just don't want to deal with all of the problems. I want some peace and quiet."

"This is all momentary, and this too shall pass. You have not been keeping up with your astrological studies, or you would know that right now, the shift in planetary alignment with the moon's entry into Pisces can lead to miscommunications of catastrophic proportions. Silence your negativity, and stay strong." Ivy held Veronica's hands and looked into her eyes steadily. Then, she gave her a hug and left to adjust her plans.

Ivy considered it critical to ensure that Veronica was not implicated in the poisoning of Josh. She needed to divert the police from the estate. Knowing that Lily was asleep at her house and Denny was out on assignment for the local news station, she immediately went to Denny's apartment and using the set of keys she took from Lily, she let herself in, quickly placed a gallon of antifreeze in his kitchen under the sink. She also hid several cases of green Gatorade far back in the kitchen pantry. She would see how the investigation unfolded over the next few days, and, if necessary, she would phone the police anonymously with a tip. If they got too close to Veronica or Lily, she would be able to tell them she'd heard of the poisoning and believed she knew who might be responsible. She could easily make up a story about overhearing Denny threatening Lily's father months ago because he wouldn't find a job for him at the family biotech company. This would serve as her backup plan.

Denny was becoming a distraction anyway, and Lily had the most important opportunity of her life coming soon. Her chances for winning the show were at stake. Lily must become famous in order for Ivy to succeed. Otherwise, Lily would become dispensable, and as much as Ivy loved her, she may not be able to save her from the others. There were larger implications from the Eristocrats if her study failed. It might unleash a chaos that would be unstoppable. Some things were simply out of her control. Such was the nature of chaos.

20

Clues

Ella started her day as usual, early at the hospital, but when she walked into her office, she was startled to find a gentleman in a ball cap, sunglasses, and jeans sitting there.

"You're late," he said as she entered slowly.

"I'm sorry, did I have an appointment that I missed on my calendar?" she asked.

"No, just shut the door behind you. We need to talk about Cole."

Ella closed the door promptly as the man removed his sunglasses so she could see his eyes. She recognized him immediately. It was Jack standing right in front of her. "We need to talk. Did you find anything at his house? Were Dr. Michaels and you able to look around?" he asked very seriously.

Ella was shocked. She thought he was in California. "Yes, but I'm afraid there wasn't much there. We didn't find anything helpful."

"Are you sure?" he asked impatiently.

"Well, the only strange thing I found was a baby sock in his dresser," she said as she pulled the sock from her purse.

Jack hesitated for a moment. "Actually, that's more important than you know." He took the sock, and as he stared at it, he told her about his discovery in California.

"It turns out that the people who want Cole dead aren't after him because of his drug dealing. Yes, they are heavily involved in the drug business, but what he did was far more dangerous than just dealing drugs."

"More dangerous? What could he have possibly done to be wanted dead by these people?" she asked.

"Well, it seems he got the boss's daughter pregnant. One of the big drug lords from Mexico lives in California now, and his daughter had the baby about six months ago. It appears that Cole is the father. I wasn't sure if he even knew about the baby, but since he had this sock, he must have known. He must have seen the baby, and he probably knows where he is. So, now they want him dead, but first, they want to find the baby and the daughter. Since she is the boss's only daughter, and she's seventeen, he's furious that she's disgraced the family. He thinks Cole must have taken advantage of her or forced himself on her."

"So, where's the baby now? And where is the daughter? Does she know Cole is in the hospital? Do the dealers know?" Questions spun through Ella's mind and spewed out of her mouth rapidly.

"That's the biggest problem. No one seems to know where the baby is. The boss man knows Cole is in the hospital. He won't have him killed if he's in a coma, and he can't find his grandson. If there's a chance Cole knows something or has the baby in hiding, he's safe until they get to talk to him and get the baby boy back. That's why he can't come out of the coma. You have to protect him until I find that baby," he explained with fear in his eyes.

"Well, we have a few more days before the week is over. I don't know what else to do after that."

"You'll find a way. Dr. Michaels will help you. You must wait until I have that baby. If they find the baby first, Cole will surely be killed. I promise, I'm a good detective, and I will find the boy," Jack assured her as he left.

21

A Dilemma

Ella was even more concerned now that she knew there was a missing baby. She was also quite worried about her own family issues. Although her dad was safe and sound in the hospital, the unknown poisoner frightened her. Of course, her mother was a suspect, but it didn't seem likely that she would go to that much trouble no matter how angry she may have been with her husband. She simply didn't have enough to gain from his death, and she didn't really seem to care enough to go to the trouble of poisoning him. It would hardly be worth her efforts, and she had given no indication that they would ever divorce. She needed the family connection and the status, which would be lost without him. It didn't matter though. Veronica would still be under suspicion.

It was getting late in the day, and Ella needed to visit her mother to give her an update on her father's status in person. There, she also could catch up with Lily. Ella still didn't know she'd moved in with Denny and hadn't had time to talk to her after their father was admitted to the hospital. She also didn't realize the police had already been investigating the estate and that her family's story was headlining the news at that moment.

As she pondered what Jack had told her, she entered the parking garage to get her car. After she pulled out her keys from her purse and before she knew what happened, two men quietly came up from behind her. One of them placed a chloroformed towel over her face, and she was knocked out cold.

After several hours, Ella slowly awakened. She opened her eyes to find her wrists tied to the arms of a dining room chair, her feet tied together, and her mouth covered by tape. She began to get her senses back, and while she had trouble focusing, she could see a blurry figure. It looked like a man with a long beard, sunglasses, and a fedora on his head. She could feel him caressing her hand. Her head was pounding.

"Ella, Ella, Ella, finally you join us. You've been out for a long time. I am sorry about the pain you must be suffering right now, but you and I need to have a little chat." He spoke softly and kindly and was still caressing her right hand. "Your hands are so important, aren't they? These are the instruments with which you save people. You must have done a very good job on Cole's surgery, don't you think? I'm sure you would agree."

Ella was so confused; she didn't know what to think. She tried to focus on what he was saying. She could see that the beard was a disguise. As she glanced around a bit, it was dark, but she could see she'd been there before. This was Cole's house where she had come with Dr. Michaels.

He smiled and held her hand with just a bit of force. "Well, my dear, you have a decision to make. Cole's spent enough time sleeping. You did a good job on his operation, so let's bring him back to the real world. I give you the choice—either your father or Cole. We have access to both of them. It's your decision."

"We want Cole, but if you disagree, we will finish off your father. Seeing as how your mother is the primary suspect in his poisoning, you also will lose her—off to jail she will go. Hmmm, that would be sad, wouldn't it?" He spoke slowly, hesitating to let her head catch up to what he was saying. "Or you can simply take Cole out of the coma so we can talk to him. We don't want to hurt him. We don't need to hurt him, but we do need to know where that baby is. We need to know what he knows—if anything. It's really very simple. No harm will come to Cole, but time is of the essence."

Ella understood exactly what he was saying. He was quite well spoken and polite for a thug. She felt stupid for coming to that house and for getting involved. She had compromised her integrity and her role as a physician by agreeing to leave Cole in a coma in the first place. The consequences were her own fault— her karma. Ella agreed to take Cole out of the coma, and the man left her, telling her she would be free within the hour.

Exactly one hour later, Dr. Michaels came to the house to find her. He cut off the ropes, and she told him what had happened. Of course, her kidnappers knew he would be there and they knew she would talk to him.

22

The Crush

Ella finished the final paperwork at the hospital with the help of Dr. Michaels, so the medications could be withdrawn. Now, Cole could slowly come out of the coma. It would still take time—probably all day. Then, he would wake up, and they would be able to evaluate him. Ella didn't know what would happen after that. There would be a strict limitation on visitors. There was no way anyone except family would be allowed to speak to him. She didn't know how those thugs thought they would be able to question him. She also didn't know how to find Jack or how to communicate with him about what had happened. All she could do was wait—wait for Cole, wait for Jack's next call, and wait to see what the kidnappers would do.

She was still shaken from what had occurred. She thought about her family and how everyone suddenly seemed so vulnerable. She needed to be sure her father was well protected and then tell her mother what had happened. First, she decided her father should leave the hospital. The easiest thing to do was to have him admitted into a high-security clinic in Colorado. He was going through the same type of treatments as that of an addict in order to rid his body of toxins. This would keep him safe, and his body could continue to heal. She made the arrangements for his immediate transfer, and Dr. Michaels agreed to fly there with him to get him settled and check out the security measures that were in place.

With that done, Ella called her mother to tell her about the kidnapping, but she downplayed it so as not to alarm her. Then, she explained why she was moving her father. Her mother proceeded to fill her in on Lily's moving in with

Denny, the ongoing investigation at the estate, and Ivy's revelation that Lily believed Veronica was the one who had caused their father harm. However, she neglected to tell Ella about the explicit photos that caused Lily to think such terrible things about her mother in the first place. Veronica did admit that she needed to work on her relationship with Lily and said Ivy would help counsel them. She convinced Ella to come back and stay at the estate. Ella had planned on staying there anyway. She definitely didn't want to be alone.

A little later, Ella received a call. Although the call came in on her office phone—not her cell—she was hoping it would be Cole's father, but the caller was a woman. "Hi, Ella, this is Sara Wagner, um, your cousin. I know it's been a while. Do you remember me?"

Ella thought for a second and yes of course she remembered her. They had been quite close as children though it had been so long ago.

Sara continued, "Anyway, somebody found your sister's wallet in the dumpster behind my work. I saw it and recognized the ID. I also saw you the other day at the press conference about Cole, so I dialed the hospital and found you. I thought you could get in touch with Lily about it."

Once Oliver discovered he had Lily's bag and realized she must have his, along with the drugs he was carrying, he knew he couldn't admit they had switched bags. Oliver lived with his sister, Sara, but didn't want her to know he had screwed up and lost the drugs. He conjured up the story about finding the wallet in the dumpster, knowing Sara would take care of it.

Ella was confused as to why Lily's wallet was missing, but she replied, "Well, thank you. I didn't know she was missing it, but I'm sure she will be happy to know you found it. So, how are you, and how's the rest of your family?" They hadn't seen each other since high school. Ella wasn't really sure what had happened between their families, but she remembered being close to her cousins at an early age, then they stopped seeing them as they got older.

"They're good, and I'm good too. I'm working at the brewery, and I recognized Lily's picture on the ID. Small world, I guess. I can drop it off at the hospital if that's OK," she said. "And, I was just wondering—I saw you on the news. You're treating Cole, and he's been a friend of mine. I've been really worried. Can you tell me anything about how he's really doing? Maybe you could let me come see him."

It certainly is a small world, Ella thought. She wondered how they knew each other. Were they old friends or new friends, and did she know about his drug dealing? Was she part of it? Ella had no idea what kind of person Sara was now, but she was curious to see her and even more curious about her relationship with Cole.

Ella asked Sara to bring Lily's wallet to the hospital later in the afternoon and told her she would try to arrange a visit with Cole. Sara arrived shortly after their call. They talked in her office for over an hour. Sara remembered spending time as children together and though it had been such a long time ago, she felt at ease and safe talking to Ella. Sara explained how she dealt a little bit of dope—only marijuana—to make some extra money and said she sold it to friends or people she knew very well. Cole used to come into the brewery where she worked and they became close, just as friends, although he had a crush on her, and Sara knew it. She took advantage of him when she needed some extra help. She just asked him to run some small errands when she was stuck on a long shift at work. He would deliver the drugs and bring her the cash. She would give him a nice tip for his help. She genuinely cared for him, but he was more like a brother.

Sara didn't go into all of details or just how the operation worked but she really didn't even know all that much. She had no idea who she was selling drugs for or who was in charge of the drugs. All she knew was that she was allowed to purchase five pounds at a time. She would send a simple text: 5@SLW (her initials) to a certain phone number. Someone would text back with a location, and Sara would receive a key via courier or FedEx within twenty-four hours.

Common locations for picking up the drugs included gym lockers, mailboxes at abandoned homes, and hotel rooms. There was never a meeting with another person, and the phone numbers changed each time there was a new delivery. The new number would be written on the package that Sara picked up, and she left cash in its place. Sara would divide her purchase and sell it to those she knew. Usually, five pounds would last her about a month. Her brother did the same thing, but he made a lot more money at it by selling a variety of club drugs like acid and Ecstasy in the places he worked as a DJ.

Cole was simply a runner, and she didn't have to pay him very much. Sara said she had been feeling sick with guilt since his arrest. She cried as she told Ella everything. She had wanted to tell the police it was all her fault, but Oliver convinced her not to confess. He said there was no sense in two people going to jail and that Cole would never do any serious jail time since he "had a screw loose" as he put it.

As they were talking, Ella got the call from the nurse that Cole was awake. She told Sara to stay put, and she ran down the hall to examine him. His eyes were just slits, but he was blinking and squinting trying to see. Ella told him to stay quiet and not to speak. She was scared about what might happen and just how those men who had kidnapped her planned to contact him. He was under heavy security, and there were cameras throughout the hospital, but she knew they would try to get to him.

As his eyes adjusted, she explained to him where he was and what had happened. She asked him to blink twice if he understood what she was saying. He did. While there was no one else in the room, she asked him if he knew there were people after him. He blinked twice. She asked if there was a baby somewhere that was his. He blinked twice. She asked him if he knew where the baby was. He blinked twice. Then, the nurses came in, and she quickly went back to her exam.

Little did she know, the men who had kidnapped her had placed a bug in a planter to listen to everything that was said. The card attached stated that it was from the headquarters of the Special Olympics. The kidnappers knew it was just a matter of time before Ella got the information they needed on the location of the baby. They knew she would ask him about it. All they had to do was wait and listen. Ella would do their work for them and lead them straight to the baby.

23

A Fine Wine

D r. Michaels had been on leave from the hospital all week and hadn't had one moment to enjoy his time off. It had been a busy few days for him, trying to help Jack, rescuing Ella, and flying out for the day to get her dad settled in Colorado. He had been hoping to spend some of his time off simply relaxing and enjoying that nice mansion that was in Cole's name. When Jack asked him to check it out and see what he could find, Dr. Michaels thought it would be a great place to enjoy. Jack, however, had failed to mention that some thugs just might drop by, and, oh yeah, they might be angry. Then, they might kidnap Ella, and to top it all off, they might be out to kill him too. He had nothing to do with the missing baby, but they didn't know that.

Dr. Michaels was annoyed. Jack had asked for his help but gave no indication of the level of danger that was involved, so when he opened his kitchen pantry, he felt no guilt about getting out that case of wine he had taken from the wine cellar back at Cole's mansion. He was going to open it and enjoy it. He had come across a variety of wine in the cellar. The cases were covered in dust and surrounded by empty packing boxes. Concern for his expensive suit led him to choose the least dusty case. He had hoped he'd grabbed one that was a leftover vintage case that had aged nicely and would be worth quite a lot. As he cracked the wood on the case, it opened easily. It was unmarked, so he thought this mystery case would be an interesting find. He was imagining the case had belonged to some wealthy old high-society gentleman from many years ago, long before drug dealers took over such a lovely residence.

He pulled out one of the bottles to take a look at his treasure. He looked over the label, and much to his shock and disgust, it was a case of ice wine! That repulsive syrup was certainly no treasure to him. It shouldn't have even been in a case sitting warm in the basement—ice wine must be kept cold at all times.

He pushed his emotions aside and pulled out each of the bottles to see if they were all the same. As he removed them from the case, he discovered a piece of paper stuck to the bottom of one of the bottles. It was a photo with a beautiful view of a vineyard at sunset, and on the back, there was a baby's footprint with a heart that simply said *Always my love, Maya.*

Suddenly, Dr. Michaels knew exactly where the baby was. He had to get to Jack to tell him. He dialed the last number he had for him, but it went straight to voicemail. Jack had been switching phones frequently to avoid being tracked, so Dr. Michaels wasn't even sure the number was still correct. He was exhausted since he'd just returned from the airport two hours ago after the Colorado trip, but he knew he had to go. He immediately gathered up his small travel bag and headed out the door. Dr. Michaels had to get the girl and the baby to save Cole, Ella—and even himself.

[To Be Continued]

www.ingramcontent.com/pod-product-compliance
Lightning Source LLC
Chambersburg PA
CBHW071346130626
46556CB00005B/2049